Loonie Summer

Illustrations by Marc Mongeau

Translated by Sarah Cummins

Formac Publishing Limited
Halifax, Nova Scotia
1994

Originally published as L'été des tordus

Copyright 1993 la courte échelle

Translation copyright 1994 by Sarah Cummins

Canadian Cataloguing in Publication Data

Duchesne, Christiane, 1949-

   [Été des tordus. English]

   Loonie summer

   (First novel series)

   Translation of: L'été des tordus.

ISBN 0-88780-272-9 (pbk) — ISBN 0-88780-273-7 (bound)

I. Mongeau, Marc. II. Title. III. Title: Été des tordus. English. IV Series

PS8557.U265E8313 1994   jC843 .54   C94-950089-5
PZ7.D83Lo 1994

Formac Publishing Limited
5502 Atlantic Street
Halifax, N.S. B3H 1G4

Printed and bound in Canada

Table of contents

*To everyone who has ever had an
imaginary friend.*

Foreword

Who are the Loonies? They are five tiny little people, just three centimetres high. Their names are Elvin, Casimir, Gomeral, Apollino, and Zenon. One night Christopher Thomas found them under his pillow.

Ever since, they have lived in Chris's room. They sleep in five little beds in a cardboard box that he keeps hidden under his own bed.

Some days the Loonies get into mischief and other days they are very, very good. The Loonies are definitely loony, but their hearts are made of gold.

Chris can't imagine what he'd do without them now. They are part of his life. And the Loonies couldn't do without Chris either.

Will they stay with him for-ever? No one really knows. But for as long as they do stay, Chris will enjoy them and he'll take care of his dear little Loonies like a papa pelican looking after his baby pelicans.

1
The birthday present

This year, our school break was in February, so we were going to celebrate my birthday at the cottage. That was fine with me. In fact, it was great, because I love being out in the country with snow everywhere.

I am always astonished to discover how thoughtful the Loonies are. They said they were going to give me a wonderful birthday present, the very thing I most wanted. I don't know how they found out what I wanted for my birthday.

I do recall mentioning to my

parents, "We should think about getting some new goldfish. Maybe for my birthday?" Could the Loonies have overheard?

The week before my birthday, they were very excited, smirking and smiling, and giggling behind my back. I'm beginning to recognize the signs of my dear little Loonies cooking up some mischief.

On February 15, three days before my birthday, we left for the cottage in the middle of a howling snowstorm.

The wind was blowing so hard that the car could hardly move. It seemed as if we were driving through a wall of snowflakes. The Loonies were hidden in my pocket, with their eyes tightly closed and their

hands over their ears. Finally
we arrived at the cottage.

Despite the weather, the very
first evening I found the Loonies clambering hastily through
my bedroom window, with their
boots all full of snow.

"Don't scold us, Chief!" said
Zenon. " We'll clean everything
up. We can't explain just now.
We just had to go outside for a
bit."

"But you know how scared you are in the snow! Why did you decide to go outside?"

"Don't worry, Chief, don't worry. We got used to it."

I decided I had to spy on them. They were not their usual selves.

On February 16 I saw them pass an enormous package through the window. What had they been up to? They don't even know anyone around here!

On February 17 there was a strange smell in the room.

"Elvin, when did you last wash your feet?"

"Last night, Chief. We all soaked our feet in the tub. Soap, bubble bath, talcum powder. The works! We brought it all with us wrapped in our kerchiefs."

On the morning of my birth-day, something stank to high heaven. The Loonies jumped on to my bed, singing the Loonies' birthday song, *Ally Mally Jujube*.

They were laughing like maniacs and holding their noses.

"Chief, we've got a present for you. Here it is!"

On the floor I saw the long package they had dragged in through the window. It was beautifully wrapped in striped paper with a gold ribbon.

The smell was unbearable. It was coming from the present. Perhaps they were giving me all their old socks? I tried to smile as I unwrapped the present.

It was a salmon! A salmon that had been kept very warm in my room for the last two days. If only they had left it outside in the snow, then it might not have gone bad.

"Do you like it, Chief? It's for your aquarium! A giant goldfish. We looked, but we couldn't find any that were the right colour. Do you like it anyway?"

"Yes. Thank you. Thank you, my dear Loonies. It was very nice of you. But I don't think I'll be able to put it in the aquarium."

Surprised, they came and sat on my knee while I explained.

"First of all, fish that you put in an aquarium have to be alive."

"Oh, of course!" cried Elvin. "Why didn't we think of that?"

I told my five disappointed Loonies all about how fish live in an aquarium.

"I understand," said Gomeral. "You put the fish in the aquarium and *afterwards* you can eat them"

I couldn't really get mad. They were trying to make me happy. It was my birthday. They could learn about fish and aquariums some other time.

2
The candles

I think my birthday this year must have been doomed. After the salmon fiasco, I had to make sure I was extra kind to the Loonies. I didn't want them to feel bad.

So I decided to give them a big treat that evening. They all hopped into the pocket of my shirt. They promised to be very good and I took them to the kitchen. My parents couldn't see them.

I had all my favourite dishes for dinner: tomato pie, buttered cucumber, octopus shish-kebabs, and mocha cake. The cake was decorated with little chocolate hearts and eight tall candles.

During dinner I slipped the Loonies crumbs and morsels of food. I could hear them quietly munching away. I saved the candles from the cake, as I do every year. When my birthday dinner was over, I went to my room to play with my presents.

"That was a fine meal," said Apollino. "Especially the cake."

"Can we keep the candles, dear little Chief?" asked Elvin.

I gave them the eight candles and off they went to bed. While I was assembling the racing car I had been given, I heard a dry little cough. Those Loonies! Even though it's freezing cold outside, they insist on going out with no hats on. Now one of them had caught a cold!

Then I heard another one coughing. Then three, four, five Loonies coughing, hacking and moaning. I snatched out the box with the five little beds. The Loonies were all down on their knees, spitting and retching their little guts out. Were they choking to death?

"Elvin! What's wrong with you all?"

Elvin made faces and waved his hands at me. He couldn't speak. I clapped them on the back — not too hard, they're so little. Casimir was turning purple. It was ten minutes before any of them could say a word.

"Whatever did you give us, Chief?" croaked Zenon.

"It's horrible!" choked Casimir.

"What are you talking about? What did you eat?"

"The candles, Chief, nothing but those candles!" replied Elvin, trying to clear his throat.

The candles! All around me were tiny pieces of wax the Loonies had spat out.

"You're not supposed to eat candles!"

"Even if they taste of mocha cake?" asked Apollino.

"You're supposed to lick them off, that's all! Don't tell me that people eat candles where you come from?"

"Never!" declared Elvin. "That's because they never taste like cake."

Oh, those loony Loonies. Will I ever really understand them?

3
Summer vacation

It's not always easy to figure out how the Loonies really feel about something. They might hate something one day and find it absolutely wonderful the next.

On the last day of school I told them that we were going to the cottage for the summer. They sulked and decided not to speak to me.

This time, they really didn't want to leave. I think they are afraid of changes. But when we went to the cottage in the winter for my birthday, they had had a lot of fun.

I had to reassure them constantly before we left. They were cranky, quarrelsome, moody and spent all their time getting angry over the tiniest thing.

"Stop squabbling! I have something very important to tell you. In the country there are field mice, chickens, porcupines, skunks, bullfrogs, sheep and four horses. There are also foxes."

"Chief, you're trying to get us killed!" cried Zenon.

"No, I'm not. I've thought of a solution. You are going to live in a cage."

"Gee, why not just put us in prison?" was Gomeral's response.

He's always grumbling!

"I'll set you up in my old guinea pig's cage. It's bright

and roomy. I'll even put a mos-quito net over it so you won't get bitten. Tomorrow morning before we leave, we'll move the beds in."

"What will your parents say about all this?" inquired Elvin.

"That's my problem."

"We promise to be very good," chorused the Loonies. What great guys!

"But we like your room here," added Apollino, with tears in his eyes. "We'll miss it."

"Just wait and see. You'll love it at the cottage in the summer-time!"

* * *

"Why are you bringing a cage?" my mother asked me in the car.

"In case I catch any field

mice."

"Don't expect to bring them back with you to town," warned my father.

"Where will the field mice sleep?" asked my mother, laughing. "In those little beds?"

"That's right. I'm going to train them."

"Christopher, you know, Loonies are one thing. Trained field mice are another. I think you might be going a little too far."

The Loonies laughed and joked during the whole trip, snuggled in the bottom of my pocket. But when we got to the country, they were so impressed they fell silent.

"It's just as beautiful in the summer as it is in the winter," whispered Elvin. "But I'm a little bit scared. Don't tell anyone, but I'm always a little nervous in new places."

The cage was very big, so I wasn't worried. They would have enough room. The best place to put it was hanging from the ceiling, where the field mice couldn't reach it. But when I went to hang it up, they all began to scream!

"Chief! This is making us dizzy!"

"I think I'm going to be sick," cried Apollino.

"Chief, Elvin's turning green! What should we do?"

I gave up the plan of hanging the cage from the ceiling and just put it on the floor. So from then on I had no peace of mind. I was always afraid that some-

thing would happen to them.

We went on long walks to-gether. I took them swimming in the lake and climbing trees. We picked strawberries and learned to identify mushrooms, mosses and lichens. They had a great time.

My room in the cottage is very small. The Loonies were happy to be so close to me.

After three days, they stopped talking about town. They declared that country life was better for health, safety and happiness. Country life was wonderful! They weren't even afraid of the animals any more.

They loved it at the cottage. But I had no rest. I had to watch over them day and night. Anything might happen!

4
Midnight dip

The Loonies can be the sweetest fellows in the world. They can also scare me out of my wits.

One evening, when they were quite sure I had fallen asleep, they decided to sneak out.

In the middle of the night I was suddenly awakened by Elvin's cry.

"Help, Chief! Come quick!"

He was stretched out on the windowsill, panting and gasping. I threw open the window, leaned out, and saw the four others tumbled in an unconscious heap in the old dip-net I used to catch frogs in when I was little.

Elvin was at death's door. I revived him as best I could and laid him down in the cage.

I ran outside, grabbed the net, and picked up the other Loonies. I shook them, slapped their cheeks, pinched their noses. When they opened their eyes, I put them in my pocket and ran back into the house.

"Into bed with you!"

"Chris," I heard my mother's sleepy voice. "It's three o'clock in the morning. What are you doing up?"

"Sleeping, Mom."

That's all I could think of saying. There's no way I could explain what I was doing.

Once they were tucked in, the

Loonies told me all about it. At midnight, they had decided to go on a fishing expedition. There are some very large fish in our lake. They thought they could catch one but instead, they all fell into the water, clinging to the handle of the dip-net.

Elvin managed to fish them out one by one. With his last ounce of strength, he dragged

them back to the house

"You know, Chief, all we wanted was to catch some fish to eat."

"You're lucky the fish didn't eat you, you noodleheads!"

I saved them all. The next day all five had bad colds, that's all.

***

Once they had recovered, the Loonies wanted to go swimming ten times a day. They said they were stifling in the guinea pig cage. Elvin begged me to let them go down to the river.

"The water in the river is cooler, Chief. The lake water is much too warm."

"You've got to be kidding, Elvin. In the river, you'd all be carried away!"

"Well, what about the fish?" asked Casimir. "They do all right in the river."

"Just stop thinking about fish all the time! Every time you start talking about fish, something terrible happens. Last year it was my aquarium. This summer it was your fishing expedition! Enough now!"

But in the end I had to give in to their whims — once again!

"I'm telling you right now: you can swim, but only inside the cage. Let's move the furniture out now."

I put the five little beds on the shelf. The Loonies bundled up their things in their kerchiefs, which I put on the beds.

"You're not going to swim with all your clothes on, are

you? Take them off, you're going to be skinny-dipping."

"Chief!" they cried in unison. "No way!"

"No one will see you. This is practically wilderness here. There's no one around. Anyway, who would care about five little bare bums like yours?"

They were shocked, they were appalled, they were insulted. They were determined to protect their bums. I could laugh all I wanted. They still refused to take off their underwear.

I put the cage in the river near the shore. The water came halfway up.

"It's better in the river than in the lake!" said Casimir. "It's more fun with the current."

"This is great, Chief!" they all

shouted. "Thank you, thank you, thank you!"

They sang and swam, practised diving, tumbled and splashed, and had the time of their lives. I watched over them.

"Careful, Chief! In stories, there's always someone who sees a butterfly and decides to chase after it. He gets lost and a lot of scary things happen before it all turns out right in the end. Don't watch any butterflies, Chief!"

Well, I didn't see any butterflies. But what I did see terrified me. Upstream there was a big dam. On this particular day, someone decided to clean the screens.

All at once the river swelled up, overflowed, and swept

everything with it downstream. Before I could reach out and grab the guinea pig cage, it disappeared right in front of my eyes. I couldn't even hear my Loonies shouting. The cage was bobbing on the water like a cork, then it sank and reappeared where I least expected it.

I tried to cross over to it on the moss-covered rocks, but I slipped and scraped my hands and feet. I cried and shouted and screamed for help.

I ran wildly along the river, certain that I would never ever see my Loonies again.

* * *

I have never thought of sheep as very intelligent animals. Now I know that there is at least one

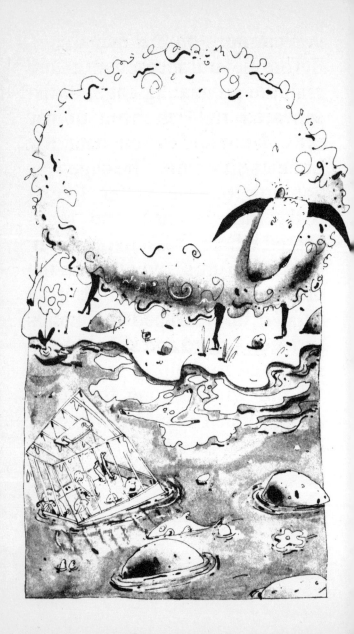

genius sheep on this earth.

This genius sheep was drinking at the riverside, a little ways downstream. The cage bounced off its head and the clever sheep nudged it up onto the bank with its nose.

The Loonies were safe and sound. They had been smart enough to cling to the bars of the cage so they wouldn't be knocked out. But every one of them had lost his undies!

5
The dog

One day I decided to teach the Loonies how to observe clouds. Since then, they've spent hours looking at the sky and have discovered all sorts of things in the clouds: giraffes, lions, elephant, and especially dogs.

"We love dogs, don't we, Zenon?" said Apollino one day while lying on his back watching the clouds.

"We don't just love dogs," answered Zenon. "We *superlove* them."

"You superlove them?"

"Yes. That's what we say

when we love something more than anything else."

"So you really like dogs, eh?"

"Oh yes," said Elvin. "Where we come from, everyone likes dogs."

I imagined that in Loonie Land, there were miniature dogs, only one centimetre high.

"Oh no, Chief!" exclaimed Zenon. "Our dogs are quite large."

"And you're not afraid of them?"

"Not at all!" said Gomeral. "Dogs are so nice."

I love dogs too. I love them so much that when I'm at the cottage, I often borrow my neighbour's dog, an enormous terrier called Lazarus.

This summer, with the Loonies

here, I hadn't borrowed Lazarus at all. He could swallow them all in a single gulp.

But since they all claimed to love dogs, I ran over to the

neighbour's house immediately. I returned in triumph, pulled along by Lazarus.

"Ta-da! Here's a dog for you all!"

The Loonies turned green with terror. Lazarus began to bark loudly. He started jumping all over, and it was all I could do to hold him back.

"It's moving! The dog is moving!" screamed the Loonies.

Moving! Of course the dog was moving! It was yelping, leaping, straining at the leash, and trying to catch the little Loonies who were running in all directions.

"Help, help! A monster! Everyone get in the cage!" cried Elvin.

I saw my chance to return the

dog to the neighbour. I would tell her why later. When I came back, the Loonies were still huddled, trembling, in their cage.

"Come on out and tell me what that was all about."

"Yes, Chief," said Elvin in a small voice.

He stepped out of the cage, peering to the left and to the right, afraid the dog might still be around.

"You see, where we come from, dogs don't move around. That's why we like them. They are big, black-and-white china dogs. They are very old, and crackled all over. One of them has even lost its tail. There are three of them. We like to climb on them. They're very slippery, and it's really fun."

Once again I realized that there are tremendous differences between the Loonies and a kid like me.

Gomeral, Apollino, Zenon, and Casimir crept out too, still shaken.

"Promise us, Chief, that the monster won't come back?"

"I promise, you poor little Loonies."

6
Parachuting

When you are no bigger than my baby finger, you are also not very heavy.

The Loonies weigh about thirty grams each, no more than a spool of thread. That's what gave me the brilliant idea of giving them parachuting lessons.

It's only about a metre from my windowsill to the ground. I often climb out through the window.

For the Loonies, it was a great adventure. They had never in their lives even heard of parachuting, and they were very excited.

Making parachutes is easy as pie. But it took at least three hours to get everything ready. The Loonies fidgeted impatiently on the windowsill.

"Are we really going to fly, Chief? Like birds, right?"

"Not exactly. What you are going to do is drift slowly down."

"But heights always make Elvin dizzy," Gomeral pointed out grumpily.

That Gomeral, he always says the wrong thing at the wrong time. But Elvin just looked at me confidently.

"Today," he announced, puffing out his chest, "I shall vanquish my vertigo! You'll see!"

Zenon went first. He made a perfect jump — flawless technique, controlled landing. Cheers all around!

When it was Gomeral's turn, Casimir couldn't resist shoving him off, which made him scream in fright. Poor Gomeral, he made a good landing, but didn't seem to enjoy it.

Apollino and Casimir couldn't keep from giggling uncontrollably. They jumped at the same time, holding hands. Their parachutes got entangled, but they landed unhurt and laughing their heads off.

Then it was Elvin's turn.

"Courage, Elvin. Don't worry. You've seen how easy it is."

"I'd like to see you try it, Chief," he muttered.

Then he jumped. But suddenly — a gust of wind lifted him high in the air, instead of letting him settle gently to the ground. Poor Elvin! Thrashing wildly about, he rose higher and higher.

He kept yelling out all the Loonie swear words he knew until finally his parachute got caught in the topmost branch of the pine tree. He refused to let me climb up to rescue him.

He managed to get free all by himself. And then, with great courage, he jumped again, from the top of the pine tree! I caught him in my hands and gave him a big hug.

As I held him close, he whispered in my ear, "Chief, heights still make me dizzy. But don't

tell the others."

He was a sickly green colour, as always when he was afraid. I had been very afraid, too. But the other Loonies didn't seem to notice. They were all clamouring for another jump.

7
The keys

"How can something just disappear into thin air?" my father shouted.

"Two sets of keys in one day! Impossible!" said my mother. "How can we go back to town without our keys? Chris, can you lend us yours?"

But I couldn't find my keys either. It was our last day at the cottage, and I didn't much feel like looking for them. I had done enough packing already.

"You can't find your keys either? No wonder. Your room is a disaster zone," said my father, closing his eyes in despair.

"My room is perfectly tidy! Can't anyone find any keys?"

My mother gave me a funny look.

"Strange, isn't it?"

I didn't answer. When strange things are happening, you can bet the Loonies are involved.

"What about our spare keys?" asked my father.

But they had disappeared too. Guess we couldn't go back to town!

I went upstairs to talk to Elvin. He wasn't there, and neither were Gomeral, Apollino, Zenon, or Casimir. Missing keys, missing Loonies. It was beginning to look a bit fishy.

What could they have done with our keys? I started to

worry. Maybe they didn't want to leave the cottage. What if they refused to return to town?

What if they had decided to run away without giving me a chance to follow them? What if they were planning some mischief to end all mischief? Would they dare to rob a bank? My heart was thudding so loudly, my ears rang.

I was trembling in fear for those horrid Loonies. How dare they spoil the last day of my vacation?

I wept with rage and worry. But when I stopped crying, I could hear the strangest music. Clenching my teeth, I climbed out the window and followed the sound, like a dog following a scent.

There they were! Hidden under the tall pine tree, their eyes closed, angelic smiles on their faces, they were playing a symphony on the family's thirty-two keys, which they had hung from the lowest branches.

The music was so enchanting that I stood stock still. I was no longer angry. Elvin winked at me. It was the most beautiful concert I had ever heard.

All I could do was tell my parents that I was to blame for the disappearance of the keys, and then have them listen to the carillon of keys, hoping that they would find it as lovely as I did. I couldn't betray my loony Loonies!

Just before the end

When it was time to go, the Loonies begged to stay. Now they really loved the countryside in summer and winter. In the country, they were never bored. In town, they often moped when it was time for me to go to school.

That night, they smiled at me as they were falling asleep, but I knew they had been crying. The pocket of my shirt, where they had spent the trip home, was all wet with their tiny tears.

Sleep well, my Loonies, and sweet dreams of summer vacation!